THE DOCTRINE OF VENUS

JAMES WOOD

The Doctrine of Venus
Copyright © 2012 by James Wood.

Edited by Sharazade for 1001 Nights Press.
Cover design by Sharazade.
Book design by Sharazade and DJ Rogers.
Cover photograph by Alfred Cheney Johnston.
Interior photographs by Jean and George Agelou.
Printed in the United States.

ISBN-13: 978-0615683850

ISBN-10: 0615683851

THE DOCTRINE OF VENUS

"I'm sorry. That book has a restricted circulation." The librarian looked down over horn-rimmed glasses, her lips twisted in a hint of a smile.

"It's for reference only," she clarified, returning it to the woman's hands.

A look passed between them for a protracted second as her customer's embarrassment grew. It seemed for a moment as if she might put the book down and flee without uttering a word, yet she clutched at the thin, worn book possessively and seemed loathe to let it go.

The librarian checked over her shoulder. There was no one else close by. "Behind you, ma'am, you'll see our local history room. It's where our archivist works. There's a photocopier there that takes coins. He goes to lunch in ten minutes time." She nodded reassuringly.

The woman hastily covered the book with her coat. "Thank you," she said. And then in a halting voice: "I don't usually read this sort of thing."

"Nobody does, ma'am. That was the idea when they banned it." And then, after a pause in which she weighed the eager look of the woman before her: "We keep all the back copies of our newspapers in the archive. October 5th, 1912, is worth a read, if this subject is of interest to you."

"October 5th?" the woman repeated.

"That's right. 1912."

"Thank you again, I'll remember that."

"But ma'am..." The librarian's tone was now cautionary, and the woman turned back to hear her out. "This sort of thing can take a hold of your life. The more you think of it, the deeper in you go. It's a bit of a rabbit hole, that's all I'm saying. If you venture inside, you may never want out."

"Thanks again," the woman said. "That's exactly what I'm hoping for."

The Grand Falls Herald
Oct. 5th, 1912
Leader - Front page

Sin and Society:
Donnell Morality Trial Verdict Delivered; More Than Eyebrows Raised

A tearful Mrs. Henry Donnell, well-known benefactress and charity champion, was escorted to a waiting car after the verdict was read out in court today. The photogenic wife of the quarry and refrigeration magnate had no comment for the press after the jury found her guilty on one charge of Public Indecency. The prosecutor had earlier withdrawn three separate charges filed under the State's Morality Code, saving Mrs. Donnell the prospect of jail time and her husband any further embarrassment.

Following sentencing, defense counsel issued a statement: "It's a private issue between husband and wife. The family considers the matter closed."

The scandal of Mrs. Donnell's relationship with Dr. Edgar Haldrew, the infamous author of *The Doctrine of Venus*, grabbed national headlines when revelations emerged of a carnal pact between the couple, based on structured principles of immoral behavior laid down in that work.

The Doctrine of Venus, a scarlet pamphlet, has been banned in forty-three states since its first publication in 1906, and recently gained renewed notoriety when a third edition went to print on the liberal presses of New England.

During the trial, the jury heard from the prosecutor: "It's a depraved book. It advocates for sinful lust and the worst of carnal perversions. Mrs. Donnell was a willing subscriber to its creed of filth. If anything, she was keener than Dr. Haldrew."

This family newspaper, in full possession of the facts of the tryst, chooses to spare the reader the sordid details. It is enough to know that the behavior of both parties in the Donnell affair is an affront to all civilized society. This esteemed journal will not slurry its name by voyeuristic indulgence in lascivious details. The *Herald* backs the call for the *Doctrine*'s full censorship, lest the institution of the American family find itself undermined by the temptations present on every page of this most wicked of books.

The Grand Falls Herald
Oct. 5th, 1912
Bottom of page one

In related news: *The Doctrine of Venus* makes bestseller list in New York, despite possession and distribution illegal, p.6. Select excerpts from the Doctrine and a "fill in the blank" competition, p.8, 9-11. "Edgar Haldrew: Beast or Beau?" Readers' wives write in, p.16. Editorial: "Wherefore our pilgrim values now? The seeds of sin in print."

The archivist checked the clock once more before he lifted the brown bag from its desk drawer. *I hate potted meat,* he thought violently, though he'd made the sandwich himself. Lorraine had been at the check out desk – that had warmed his day. He touched his crotch to make sure his fly was up and sucked in his gut a little. His preparations complete, the archivist headed to the staff room. Behind him, he heard the photocopier warm up, but he paid it no attention; his head was full of absurd plans of conquest, of derring-do and triumph.

THE DOCTRINE
OF
VENUS

BY EDGAR HALDREW, M.D.

The Doctrine of Venus

Constituting the norms, duties, and behaviors expected of a daughter of Aphrodite in America, as made relevant to the modern age.

Edgar Haldrew, M.D.

1st Ed. 1906
2nd Ed. 1908
3rd Ed. (Both amended & expanded) 1911

Preface

It being known and established, that within each human mind there exists a diametric state:

On the one side, rational Apollo governs with his structure and order and rules. He represents both safety and strength.

On the other side, passionate Bacchus is unfettered, his desires never fully slaked. He represents sensation and appetite. Appetite for pleasure.

A woman, being flesh, of Adam's rib, feels the pull of both. She is happiest when made complete, as is man, her partner in all.

The Articles of the Doctrine of Venus (numbering seven)

I. That a daughter of Aphrodite has the right to choose her lover. She must never be forced or coerced. (The Principle of Final Free Will.)

II. That upon her willing submission, her master will collar his lady.

III. That the master, by collaring her, promises his lady that he will cherish, protect, and adore her.

IV. That the lady, by her acceptance of his collar, gives her body and her passion unconditionally to him.

V. That the master has a duty to set rules for the behavior of his lady, that she may know her place and be improved by them.

VI. That erotic punishment is a necessary part of her confidence in Article V.

VII. That a daughter of Aphrodite has the right at any time to return her master's collar.

Interpretation of the Doctrine of Venus – for the benefit of the initiate

Article I: *That a daughter of Aphrodite has the right to choose her lover. She must never be forced or coerced.*

This article makes clear the principle of <u>final free will</u>. A woman, determined on the course of love of which the Doctrine speaks, has but one choice – to consent to a master or not. Her suitor should never seek to pressure her by soft words or force of hand. A woman makes her own choice of lover, and gives her informed consent.

Sober thought need precede her decision. She should not act in haste. A daughter of Aphrodite, accepting a lover, is embracing her own submission. This is the point of <u>final free will</u>, beyond which she releases control.

"How do I know a true man?" is her question. It is in her own heart to find him. She should be wary of cads, posers, and braggarts. She should be leery of all lesser men. She should take care not to value herself less than she deserves. A daughter of Aphrodite always aspires to be the best girl she can be.

Figure 1: It is in her own heart to find him.

Article II: *That upon her willing submission, her master will collar his lady.*

The matter of collars has invited much correspondence since the first edition, and the subject bears expanding upon.

The collar is, above all, a symbol: a symbol of a woman's choice to submit to her master's care.

The collar is also a totem. In it resides the spirit of both order and unchecked passion — of Apollo and Dionysus combined.

Thirdly, it is the mark of the bond between the lovers, and of the master's possession of his lady.

Heavy with symbolic weight, the collar should not be treated lightly. It is a very great day in lady's life when she accepts the collar of her lover.

∽

Most collars are a gift worn around the bare neck. A velvet choker, perhaps with a cameo, is commonly employed; while a leather collar, like one might use on a dog, is also eminently suitable.

A collar, however, is not restricted to form. While it should be worn upon a lady's body, neither its look nor its material composition is prescribed in any way.

With the symbolism of the collar stressed, a collar can be as varied as imagination permits.

Personal circumstance may make it difficult for the lady to sport her affection publicly. If she finds herself married to another, she will not wish her adultery exposed. Likewise, a maiden has good reason to keep her public reputation unsmirched. A special bracelet will do the trick, or a chain around her ankle. Hidden by a stocking, she can easily wear her collar in company.

❧

A ring is not a suitable collar, lest it be muddled with that other institution.

❧

A lady will always take pride in her collar, for it is a reflection of her master and his care for her in all things.

❧

Many questions pertaining to the observance of collar wearing have arisen since the first edition. Hypothetical rhetoric, in certain circles, has given course to heated words. Of primary issue is debate surrounding the dogma of <u>singularity</u>: the question of whether a lady may accept more than one collar at a time – either from the same master, as in a multitude of material collars, or from different masters, as in giving service to more than one master concurrently.

Let it be clear: A lady only serves one master at a time, though she may be possessed of more than one collar.

A lady in possession of many collars submits herself to the first one she puts on.

A lady may not wear the collars of two masters simultaneously.

Figure 2: A collar is the mark of the master's
possession of his lady.

Article III: *That the master, by collaring her, promises his lady that he will cherish, protect, and adore her.*

The responsibilities of a master are many and grave. The promises he makes his lady by collaring her need not be spoken, but are implicit in the act itself. This is the principle of <u>care</u>.

His lady has not only surrendered herself as an object to his carnal pleasures; she has given him, also, her complete faith and trust, and oftentimes no small part of her heart. This great responsibility is for a master to bear resolutely. He is being honored by his lady, and the faith she has shown in him, by her acceptance of his collar.

It is a master's solemn duty, under the principle of care, to make good this faith by his devotion to his lady's well-being.

He will keep her safe from all threats and worries. He will take care to guard her reputation. He will keep her secrets closer than he keeps his own. He will fight duels, if need be, for her honor. He will allow her no harm. He will defend her against physical travails and shelter her from economic storms. She is, to him, more precious than gold.

Note that punishments and corrections are not a harm or injury. Serving, as they do, the higher purpose of molding and improving a lady's character, they are a sign of his care and affection. While physical discomfort is the lot of a lady who finds herself temporarily spanked, she should tender thought to the efforts of the man whose lap she lies across and the lesson he is trying to impart. Has she been a naughty girl, or is he reminding her who is in charge? She should take succor that she has his sole attention, and be proud that she is worthy of his exertions. It is not without reason that many a lady has confessed she gets wet from these intimacies.

So it is that in word and deed, as much as in his carnal attentions, does a master show adoration of his lady.

Figure 3: He will cherish, protect, and adore her.

Article IV: *That the lady, by her acceptance of his collar, gives her body and her passion unconditionally to him.*

A collared woman seeks many things: security, protection, freedom, love, and attention. She wants to be cherished and to be taken care of, to be safe under the arm of her master. She seeks shielding from the pin-pricks of responsibility, the scratch-ing annoyance of constant trivial decision making. He takes that away from her and it is liberation for her. She finds freedom under his care. She can lean on her master's strong supportive arm. She knows he always has her very best interests at heart.

This is what opens her. This is what allows a daughter of Aphrodite to surrender her flesh, and to revel in all her desires.

Thus opened and uninhibited, she is ripe for the sensuous pleasures. It is her duty to respond to her master's advances and encourage him with her enthusiasm.

A master may whisper to his lady and encourage her to confess all her darkest desires. It is her duty to answer truthfully and fully. Often in a lady's most shameful fantasies does she find the greatest intimacy. Her confession is another bond of trust. And while no master is beholden to accommodate, it is a dim man and stale lover who passes such treasures willingly. Thus, more than one lady has found herself the living embodiment of her nightly thoughts. Whether it is being taken by more than one man at the same time; or the taboo desire of being hunted down, chased and caught, and violated against her will; or mixing her flesh with a different race or for a show to a public room – a collared lady may find she is required to participate in every detail of her own forbidden dreams.

A lady should be careful of what she secretly desires, but more careful yet not to bury it so deep that it withers in her breast unrealized.

Figure 4: Often in a lady's most shameful
fantasies does she find the greatest intimacy.

Article V: *That the master has a duty to set rules for the behavior of his lady, that she may know her place and be improved by them.*

It being the case that the volume of letters on the subject of <u>rules</u> was a match for all other correspondence combined, it would be a great disservice to the attentive reader if the matter were not expanded upon.

Further, it bears noting that not one voice was raised to challenge the need for rules, or to suggest that they were inappropriate in and of themselves. Indeed they are not, for rules form the backbone on which the Doctrine of Venus walks.

"What rules should be applied?" That question was heard most. The simple answer is this: "Whatever rules work for you." But the baying of the eager initiate will not be parlayed so easily. The student of the Doctrine of Venus demands a fuller answer.

The master's rules are the architect's drawings from which their relationship is built. Remembering this at all times, and bowing to the reader's privilege, a list of examples that may serve as rules now follows for the initiate.

⌒

A set of rules, very commonly, will include references to <u>deportment</u>. A master will very often hold an opinion of how he wishes his lady to look and present herself.

The state of her corsetry, the height of her heels, the fashion and color of her dress, the style of her hair and make-up – these are often specified by a master, and his lady will take pleasure in complying.

A daughter of Aphrodite takes great pleasure in being pretty for her man. His compliments warm her. She takes pleasure in making him happy. He will often buy her the fashions he fancies and, over time, furnish her with a complete wardrobe, each piece therein carefully selected according to his taste and pleasure.

Rules of deportment may cover more intimate items or pertain to specific occasions. The donning of costume in bedroom play is not unknown to many. A master may have fancy to jewelry of an intimate nature that his lady will be required to wear. Specialty items that rest in a lady's cavities can be found for purchase, or ordered to commission, in many of our larger cities. At a party, a master may take his lady aside and insert such items himself.

His rule may require her to engage with the company while carrying such toys within her.

Rules of deportment may also extend to particulars of the lady's intimate grooming. A master may make merry in his lady's natural state, and he may forbid her to shave whatsoever. A forest of armpit hair may be culturally arousing to him.

Another man may yet take a contrary view, and his rules will reflect this. Once again, it is his lady's pleasure to oblige him. She may find he insists on wielding the soap brush and razor himself, to relieve her of unwanted hair.

Bathing together, and mutual attention to such ablutions, is an endearment. She will grow closer to him because of it.

He may brush her hair or braid it to his style; he may perfume her or dress her himself.

A lady should view these attentions for what they are: thoughtful, intimate, and to be cherished.

∽

Figure 5a: A daughter of Aphrodite takes great
pleasure in being pretty for her man.

Some rules speak to a lady's manners – how he wishes for her to behave.

A master takes great pride in his lady and will wish her to be polite in all things.

A set of rules is not complete without reference to appropriate names. Ritualized titles lend bricks to the house of the lovers' play.

A master will often require his lady to address him in a specific fashion. It is common that a form of address will be particular to the given situation. Certain names for public; different names in private.

According to his taste, he may require her to use his Christian name, or alternatively insist on his surname always. "Yes, Mr. X." It is the master's choice, and the lady's pleasure to comply.

In private, he may have her call him "Sir" or "My Lord" or even "Master." Each time she says it, the habit builds and reinforces her submissive state.

A master should make a name for his lady, as if he were taking a pet; "my girl," for example, or "kitten" if she is the purring type. It should be a special name for her alone, and she will grow to cherish it.

A master may find that his lady responds favorably to the employ of foul-name calling. It may please him to indulge her. A lady, schooled by society to be shamed by such terms, may squirm and writhe under the hot breath that speaks them into her ear: "whore," "harlot," "wench." While her ears blush, her body is warmed, and her master knows the truth.

Dirty talk, in the application of names, is very effective when it is re-communicated. A lady who squirms when called dirty names will find the sensation re-doubled by being forced to speak. A master who doubts the veracity of this statement should try the following example: Tie the lady up, and while stimulating her by hand, whisper in her ear, "You are my whore." Then ask her what she is, and whose she is. Make her say it out loud. Very few ladies brought to release in such a circumstance will deny an emotional charge.

Rules on names are often guided by experience, and it is common for them to evolve.

❧

While it is true that the bulk of rules are often bent to matters of a sexualized nature, this need not and should not constitute their entirety. The Article is clear that rules are for a lady's improvement. This can take a multiplicity of forms beyond that solely of carnal appetite.

Rules of improvement may extend to the arts, reading, hobbies, making friends, and increasingly, success in the workplace. Many a lady has mastered the piano after her master made a rule to her practicing. Rules insisting on fresh air, long walks, correspondence with relatives, regular sleep, or the moderation of libation are not unknown; and when appropriately applied – as all rules should be – are always to the lady's improvement.

It is hoped that this great nation will soon see the sense of admitting to all women the suffrage. An amendment to the constitution cannot be far away to grant that right first enjoyed in Wyoming.

The Doctrine, like the vote itself, is emancipating. A lady, through her observance of it, can be happy and better herself.

❦

Rules should be put in place that govern <u>availability</u>. A daughter of Aphrodite likes nothing better than to be told that she is open for his pleasure.

If there are children or servants in the household, there may be rules prohibiting play in the absence of privacy.

A common rule is one that states that while in private the lady is at her master's convenience. It will specify that she may not refuse her master's advances, save for illness or specified health reasons. Furthermore, it will often state clearly that he can make free with any part of her body. She has given herself to him in her entirety, body and soul. This is what wearing his collar means, and he should take care that he regularly enjoys his use of her.

Nothing reminds a lady that she is collared like being taken by her man. To be laid down on the floor, or thrown onto the bed, or pushed down over the kitchen table; to have her clothes torn away from her body; to be held down for his appetites – this lets her know she is desired and beautiful; she does not doubt why she wears his collar.

If the rule states that she is available to him utterly, then he should not approach her like a minister or a lamb. Rather, like a rutting goat, he should have her womanhood regularly; but more than this, he should spend time within her mouth and between her breasts, and take her anally also. She should not be able to go to sleep and think: "There is a part of me he does not know."

A master that takes his lady utterly is not only rewarded in the moment. He will smile as she crawls to his side and curls up snug under his arm.

Many lovers who subscribe to the Doctrine of Venus are not able to spend continuous time together. One rule that helps overcome this separation is often termed <u>The Offering</u>. When formalized, it also serves to reinforce <u>availability</u>.

The Offering in its common form takes a pattern similar to this example: First thing every morning, the lady, ensuring she is wearing her collar, will go down on her hands and knees. She may do this on her bed, or the floor of her bedroom; or if she is not at liberty to explain her behavior, then she may retreat behind the locked door in the powder room.

Once she is in this position, she will lift the hem of her nightdress. She now lowers her shoulders so that her exposed backside sits up invitingly into the air.

With her knees spread, she is striking a tempting pose that will lure her master if he is present. If her lover is absent, her thoughts turn to him as she speaks the next part of the ritual.

She speaks, if only in a whisper, a mantra her master has prepared for her. She is often required to put her hand over her mons as she repeats a simple phrase: "I give my body to you, Master. Use me as you wish." It is this or something similar.

The collared lady should hold her provocative pose for about ten full seconds. The morning has only just begun, and yet her feminine desires are awoken. If her master is absent, he may require that she now masturbate before breaking position. The day that stretches before her has a glow to it already.

In this way she has completed The Offering.

Such rituals build on each other and help define the secret life the lovers are building together.

❧

Figure 5b: "I give my body to you, Master.
Use me as you wish."

An effective and simple rule, and one that can be played out in public without fear of discovery, is the <u>ritual of tea</u>.

Tea or coffee, or something stronger, whichever the master prefers, will be prepared by his lady and brought to him by her in a special cup that she bought for the purpose.

This is a time for her to show her master her compliance with <u>deportment</u> and <u>manners</u>. She stands beside his chair while he drinks, and waits until he is finished.

The ritual will perhaps allow him to run a hand up her leg while he is drinking, or to intrude his fingers inside of her underwear and trace the contours of her petals.

She suffers his pleasure until he is finished, and then she takes his empty cup away, puts on an apron, and cleans it for his use later.

In a public setting, when the lady fetches tea for company or has it ordered in a hotel, her head becomes full of the hidden associations. Like a cat at the door, her body will mew for the attention it knows she is missing.

The repetition of such small, but detailed, ritualized affections is the mortar of their relationship.

❧

Another common rule will pertain to

<u>inspection</u>. A master, especially one who has laid out <u>deportment</u> rules, should take care to ensure his rules are followed. Inspection lets him do that.

He should take the time to pose his lady and make her stand still while he inspects her. She will welcome his compliments and take pride in his satisfaction, and value the attention and time he devotes to her. He is showing her his rules are not trivial.

He should be thorough. He should make his lady lift her dress or stand still while he does so himself. He should unbutton her blouse and pay attention to what she has on underneath. An arrangement of mirrors makes this task easier for the master and leaves his lady in no doubt about his scrutiny.

He might straighten the seam on her stocking or re-adjust a garter clip. He may hide the label of her brassiere after tightening an errant shoulder strap.

Paying attention to her in this fashion, while she is made to pose with her hands at her sides, is a tease or a comfort to a collared lady, but in either case it assures her that *he* is paying her the keenest attention. His touches do not go unnoticed.

A rule to foster intimacy and reinforce <u>submission</u> is one usually termed <u>service</u>. Service requires a daughter of Aphrodite to go down on her knees for her master.

This common rule has the lady take her man into her mouth every day. The master need not necessarily be firm, or desirous of fellatio or congress of any sort.

The master usually stands while his lady goes to work. She sinks to her knees or squats on her heels and puts her hand upon his thigh. The master may unbutton himself, but it is better for their bonding if she does so. His lady then retrieves his girth from her master's shorts and holds it at first in her hands.

As it hangs near her face she may look on it before opening her lips to claim it. There, cradled between her cheeks and tongue, she feels her master well with the world. His amiable look tells the lady she has served her master well. He may stroke her hair or grip it tightly, according to his preference. He may insist on constant eye contact.

Ten or twenty seconds will be enough to tell her if she should per-form any further service. If the ritual is done last thing before sleep, she can rest knowing that she has been a good girl.

Like the rules of <u>offering</u>, the physical intimacy of <u>service</u> works over time to help forge a bond between the two lovers.

$$\backsim\!\!\!\sim$$

The rule of <u>cleaning</u> is also assisted by a lady's comfort in rules of <u>service</u>.

This is not to be confused with common household chores — a master should at all times employ a maid, and spare his lady a life of drudgery.

<u>Cleaning</u> is a rule that requires a lady to use her mouth following her master's attentions.

While it is true that following the cessation of coitus he may rest a while inside her cavity, eventually he must regrettably withdraw, and his pride will be stained with their fluids.

It is a lady's job to follow the rule of cleaning and polish him till he sparkles. She should commonly employ no other tools than her tongue along with her mouth and her abundant enthusiasm.

A lady knows by the seed swimming inside her belly that she is cared for and valued and cherished.

$$\backsim\!\!\!\sim$$

These are examples of rules under the Doctrine for the assistance of curious readers.

Figure 5c: He should make her stand still
while he inspects her.

Article VI: *That erotic punishment is a necessary part of her confidence in Article V.*

The nature of what is meant by "erotic punishment" need not be entered into within this text. Intelligent adults, from which pool many observants of the Doctrine of Venus are drawn, are more than capable of visualizing and creating their own cherished punishments.

It would be frippery to enunciate on the possibilities, but summoning your lady and making her lie over your lap while you administered her a sound spanking would likely be included on a redundant list of that sort.

A daughter of Aphrodite understands her master is in charge, but it is no wasted effort to make that dynamic clear through regular attention to her backside.

A lady who is put over her master's knee and has her skirts lifted knows her place and cherishes it. The feel and sound of his strong hand as it resounds off her pert bottom leaves her little room for doubt.

It is no bad thing if she struggles

a little, since it confirms for her how powerless she is. By holding her wrists as he lifts her petticoats, he can allow her to kick her heels with no chance of escape.

⤜⤛

It is important to maintain a clear distinction between <u>corrective</u> and <u>endearment</u> punishment.

The former, corrective punishment, is required following a transgression of rules, where the sentiment "a bad girl gets exactly what she deserves" applies.

A lady may obtain a spiritual and physical pleasure from even knowing that a list of punishments exists. She enjoys the rules and structure her master provides her, and corrective punishment make them real. A rule transcends from theory to form through the introduction of the whip.

The latter, endearment punishment, is a punishment that is regularly scheduled. Such punishments should be given no less frequently than once per month, thereby ensuring their efficacy.

It is important that a time of day, or a day of the week, or a day of the month is made and kept for such punishments.

A daughter of Aphrodite often finds the inevitability of such correction stimulating. No matter how good a girl, or how obedient or attendant she has been, she still knows her master's attentions are forthcoming. She reads it on the calendar. There is no hope of escape or reprieve.

The master should make it clear to his lady that she bears no fault, but that it is inevitable according to her situation. This assurance will serve to lessen her guilt and help her free herself to surrender to it.

A master may decide not to call such touches 'punishment.' The word 'correction' is widely employed.

The reader is not likely interested in the details of preparation: the choice of a favorite riding crop; the selection of a flat backed hairbrush; the cutting and testing of a flexible switch newly pruned from the branch of an apple tree.

The reader, likewise, will bear little interest in how a master might arrange his lady: bent across the back of a couch or chair; tied and suspended from a roof beam; spread-eagled on the conjugal bed.

The reader will almost certainly not be bothered by the particulars of the lady's situation: whether she is made to arrive naked for the occasion, or is stripped by her master during it; whether she is made to wear the underclothes of a Jezebel or is painted with a whore's face; whether her punishment takes place in private seclusion or in front of an audience of friends.

None of this sort will interest the reader who must devise for themselves their own pleasures.

❧

During her correction, it is important that the lady be touched with regularity, and often in an intimate way. If this pattern is repeated, she will soon find that a dampness comes of itself by the mere thought, sight, or sound of a favorite instrument employed during her correction. Even a picture. This is most satisfactory to master and lady both.

❧

Do not underestimate the value of shame as a source of exquisite pleasure. A lady will much be reduced to squirming by the application of choice coarse names. She is particularly susceptible to such conversation when it is whispered as she is held.

A lady who is made to expose herself for her master, or one who is made to stand in a corner with her underwear down, or one who is made to squat and make water into a chamber pot, or one who is made to speak out loud and admit to salacious desires, likewise revels in the torments of shame.

Punishment or correction, ultimately, is about training.

A master's job is to make his lady the best woman she can be. The master's rules are the tools by which he lets his lady flower. Rules convey to the daughter of Aphrodite security, stability, and freedom. In this light, his punishment for transgression is nothing less than a kindness.

Figure 6: A bad girl gets exactly what she deserves.

Article VII: *That a daughter of Aphrodite has the right at any time to return her master's collar.*

Read together with Articles I and IV, Article VII makes it clear that the return of a collar sunders the relationship and returns to the woman her free will.

There has been much nonsense written about this; journeymen lawyers and other such blowhards make much game of the contorted possibilities.

The spirit of the article is clear: The lady at all times holds the choice – to wear his collar or not.

It is not necessary that a lady wear her collar all day and night. She puts it on as she wishes.

Nor is she dissolving her relationship by temporarily removing her collar.

Furthermore, a collar 'returned' need not be physically handed over to achieve that state and title. Should a master refuse receipt of a returned collar, he has not affected the outcome; and is lowlier than a worm besides.

A lady may, of her choosing, maintain a collection of collars of past lovers to whom she no longer submits; her notice of their 'return' being presumably written or verbal.

Why might a woman return her collar? The reasons may be as numerous as leaves in a forest, and more colorful besides. Dissatisfaction with his attentions is an obvious reason, or guilt, or new feelings for another.

A master may request the return of a collar, and by doing so cast his lover out.

⌒〜⌒

As the <u>Rule of Singularity</u> makes clear, a woman may wear only one collar at a time. If she temporarily puts down the collar of one master, she may take up the collar of another.

Circumstances, as numerous as grains of sand upon a beach, and oftentimes more coarse, can be envisaged where this is appropriate. One master may be away a while at sea, or grown old and be physically past it. Or her energies may be such that she enjoys, even revels in, the attentions of multiple spears. The reasons are hers solely to divine, providing the Rule of Singularity is not breached.

⌒〜⌒

Collared women need not surrender their title upon being widowed from

their master, though they may do so if
they wish.

❧

Here ends *The Doctrine of Venus* in
its authorized 3rd edition.

Figure 7: The lady at all times has the choice
to wear the collar or not.

Note from the Publisher to the 3rd edition:

All correspondence pertaining to *The Doctrine of Venus* should be entered into with the author or his agent directly. The company maintains a strict policy of shredding all prurient material before it is opened.

Not for sale or distribution outside the State of Connecticut.

"Why did you do it, Vanessa? How could you do that to me?"

The car gained speed rapidly once it was clear of the crowd on the street.

"I want a divorce, Henry. There's really nothing to say."

She crossed her legs, and her stockings shimmered as they caught the light from the afternoon sun. The driver adjusted his mirror.

"You're going back to him? Jesus, Vanessa. Is that what you're telling me now?"

Mr. Donnell was older, and looked near to bursting a blood vessel. A red face under cropped snowy hair; eyes unaccustomed to kindness.

"Going back?" Mrs. Donnell looked amused. "I never left him, Henry. What did you think? Did you believe that none of it was real?"

"That Edgar Haldrew... I'll ruin the man!" he sputtered. "Just tell me, doll. Make me understand. What has he got that I don't give you?"

Heading down the coast road, the driver stole glances at Mrs. Donnell. The dark-haired beauty in the rear-view mirror kept toying with her ornate bracelet. She wasn't replying to her husband's badgering, which was a charity of a sort.

I bet she could tell a story... but at that moment a blaring horn jarred his thoughts, and his mind swerved back to the road.

The last of the public were leaving the library. The stragglers lined up at the check-out desk. Lorraine stood with her keys, guarding the door, turning the late-comers away.

"I'm sorry. We're just closing up. We're open to-morrow at nine."

Her cell phone chimed. A message was waiting. She felt a rush of expectant desire.

"Could you take care of the door?" she asked a colleague. "I've forgotten something in the back."

Lorraine made her way to the bathroom and removed her panties, as the text had instructed her to do. She lifted her skirt above her hips and then slipped them down over her garters. She reached up a hand to the black beaded necklace that fit snugly around her throat. She closed her eyes and fingered its dimples as if she were counting a rosary. *Remove your panties and touch yourself. You are not permitted to cum.* She obeyed, as she always did. Her free hand ran up the inside of her thigh and rested upon her mound. One finger and then two. She was soaking before she started.

Lorraine smoothed her skirt back down, covering her nakedness entirely. She balled the black lace of her underwear in her palm and zipped it into a pocket of her handbag before she left the room. She fetched her coat and returned to the front desk where the rest of the staff were departing.

His car was alone at the back of the near-empty parking lot. He did not need to park it so far away, but Lorraine knew he liked to look at her. He liked to make her walk across it as if on a stage, his eyes on her all the way, following her gait and roaming over her body with a possessive hungry look. She liked it too. She liked being wanted. She liked being desired that way. He knew she was naked underneath. He knew all of her secrets.

The door was open. He leaned over and kissed her on the mouth as she got into the seat beside him.

"How was your day, my pet?"

"It was fine, Sir, thank you."

"That's good. Please arrange your dress for me."

Lorraine hitched up her skirt just at the back so that her bare thighs and ass pressed the leather. It was the way he liked, and it felt good – both the sensation and pleasing him. She arranged her pleats so that nothing would look amiss to the eyes of the outside world. He nodded his approval.

"Put your hand on me while we drive."

She unbuttoned him as he navigated the exit and then slipped her hand inside.

"There was a lady who tried to take the book out today. You would have laughed to see her blush." She felt him swell as she squeezed him gently, the flesh of him under her fingers. The leather of her seat felt a little bit warmer against her soft bare skin.

"Oh, that's very good, kitten. Just keep doing that. And what did you do, my dear? Did you say anything to your lady customer?"

"I helped her out. She didn't look the type, if I'm being honest, but I suppose you can never tell."

"You're quite right there, darling; you never can tell. Now it's time we got you home."

THE END

James Wood's website:
http://jameswooderotica.com